Our Spec Rock Pool

written by Jay Dale
illustrated by Andrew Everitt-Stewart

Rosie and Mum were at the beach.
The sun was hot
and the sky was blue.

Dad ran up the beach.

"Come on, Rosie," he smiled.

"Are you ready to go swimming with me?"

Rosie looked at the big waves.

They went up and down.

Crash! Crash! Crash!

"No!" said Rosie.

"The waves are too big for me.

I will stay here with Mum."

Mum smiled at Rosie.
"Dad will take care of you,"
she said.

"No!" said Rosie.
"The waves will make me fall over,
and I will go under."

Dad took Rosie's hand.
"Come on," he said.
"I want to show you
a special little rock pool.
We can go swimming in it."

"Are there big waves
in the rock pool?" asked Rosie.

"No," said Dad.
"The water is very still."

9

Rosie and Dad walked slowly
along the beach.

"Look!" said Dad.

"Here is our special rock pool.

We can go swimming in here."

Rosie looked at the little rock pool.

The water was very still.

"Come in!" said Dad.

"There are no waves in here."

Rosie got into the rock pool.

The water was very still.

She went round and round.

"I'm like a little fish," she smiled.

Dad smiled, too.

"Look!" he said.

"Can you see a little fish
down there?"

"Yes!" said Rosie.
"I can see a little fish.
It's swimming like me."

"I like swimming with you, Dad,"
said Rosie.
"This is our special rock pool."